NO JUMPING ON THE BED!

*Specially for Sarah,
a professional bed-jumper!*

Tedd Arnold

NO JUMPING ON THE BED!

Tedd Arnold

Dial Books for Young Readers · New York

Published by Dial Books for Young Readers
A Division of NAL Penguin Inc.
2 Park Avenue
New York, New York 10016

Published simultaneously in Canada by
Fitzhenry & Whiteside Limited, Toronto

Design by Nancy R. Leo
Printed in Hong Kong by South China Printing Co.
W
3 5 7 9 10 8 6 4 2

Library of Congress Cataloging in Publication Data
Arnold, Tedd. No jumping on the bed!
Summary: Walter lives near the top floor of a tall apartment building,
where one night his habit of jumping on his bed leads to a
tumultuous fall through floor after floor, collecting occupants
all the way down.
[1. Apartment houses—Fiction.] I. Title.
PZ7.A7379No 1987   [E]   86-13501
ISBN 0-8037-0038-5   ISBN 0-8037-0039-3 (lib. bdg.)

The artwork was prepared using colored pencils and
watercolor washes. It was then color-separated and reproduced
as red, blue, yellow, and black halftones.

For William and Walter

Special thanks to
Peter Elek and Paula Wiseman

In his bedroom near the top floor of a tall apartment building, Walter was getting ready for bed.

Before turning out the light his father said, "If I've told you once I've told you a million times, no jumping on the bed! One day it'll crash right through the floor. Now lie down and go to sleep."

"Just one more time?" asked Walter. But instead he plopped down on his pillow and squeezed his eyes closed.

"Good night," said his father. He turned off the light and pulled the door almost closed.

The room was dark and quiet . . .

except for a soft thump, thump, thump coming from the room above.

"That's Delbert upstairs," thought Walter.

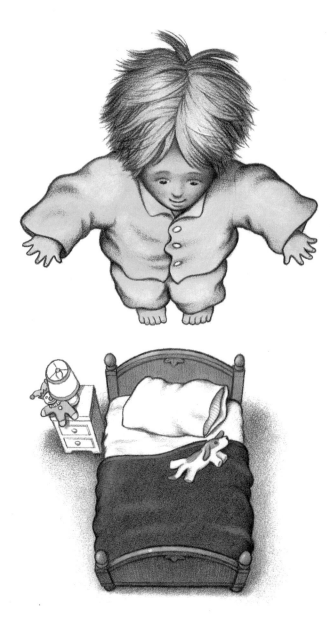

He switched on his bedside lamp. "If Delbert can jump
on his bed, so can I."

Walter bounced higher and higher. On his last jump his
hair brushed the ceiling. But when he came back down,
his mattress creaked, the floor cracked, and the whole bed
tipped sideways. Then down through the floor fell Walter,
bed and all.

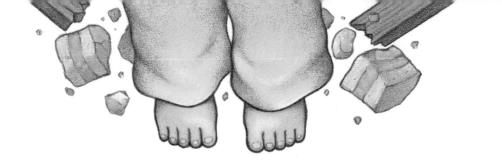

Now, it happened that Walter's bedroom was directly above Miss Hattie's dining room. She was more than a little surprised when a bed fell through her ceiling and Walter landed in her plate of spaghetti and meatballs.

"I was not expecting company for dinner!" she mumbled with a mouthful of meatballs.

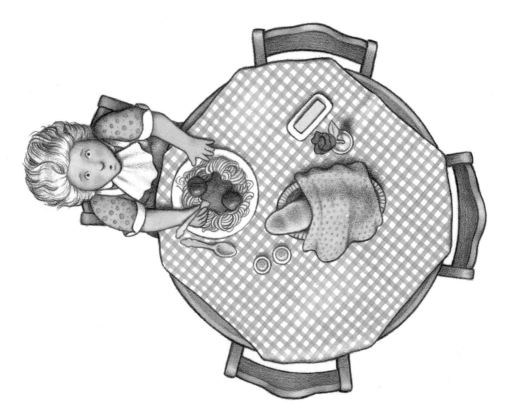

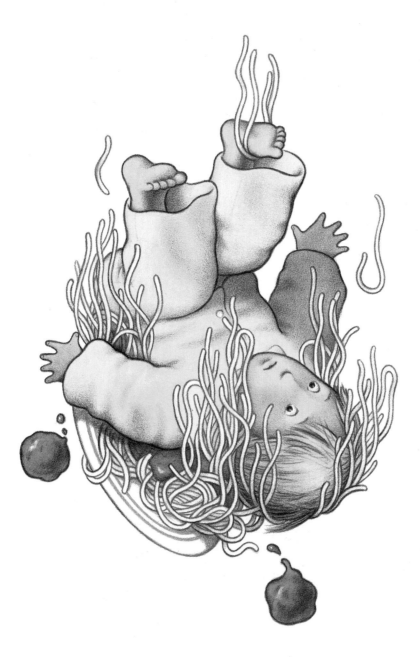

"M-m-m," said Walter, "spaghetti is my all-time favorite!"
But before he could eat, his bed smashed through the
table and kept right on crashing down through the floor.

Down and down fell Walter, Miss Hattie, the plate of
spaghetti, the bed, and all.

Miss Hattie's dining room was above Mr. Matty's TV room.
Mr. Matty didn't even notice a bed falling through his
ceiling until a meatball bounced off his head, Miss Hattie
tumbled into his lap, and Walter splashed into his aquarium.

"I've already had my bath tonight," said Walter. He wanted
to stay and watch the monsters on TV but his bed crunched
through the floor, taking the TV with it.

Down and down fell Walter, Miss Hattie, Mr. Matty, the TV, the spaghetti, the bed, and all.

Walter's Aunt Batty had just moved into the building. She was still unpacking when Miss Hattie, Mr. Matty, and a dripping wet Walter tumbled through the ceiling right into a box containing her rare Patagonian stamp collection.

When he burst through the bottom of the box, Walter was a sticky mess.

"I see you've started collecting stamps," said Aunt Batty as she followed Walter through the new hole in her floor.

Down and down fell Walter, Miss Hattie, Mr. Matty, Aunt Batty, the stamp collection, the TV, the spaghetti, the bed, and all.

Patty and Natty had worked three days building their dream house with blocks. Afraid that Fatty Cat might knock something over, they carefully shooed her out for the night. Then the upstairs neighbors came through the ceiling.

"Excuse us," said Walter, remembering his manners. "We won't be staying long."

The words were barely past his lips when Walter's bed bashed through the floor and continued on its way.

Down and down fell Walter, Miss Hattie, Mr. Matty, Aunt Batty, Patty, Natty, Fatty Cat, the stamps, the TV, the spaghetti, the bed, and all.

The last thing Mr. Hanratty ever expected to see was a bed coming through his studio ceiling, followed by nearly everyone in the building.

"If I had known you wanted to see my paintings," he said, "I would have tidied up a bit."

But they never once paused to admire Mr. Hanratty's colorful artwork. They were too busy splashing in his cans of paint. Then his floor caved in and everyone followed Walter's bed down through the hole.

Down and down fell Walter, Miss Hattie, Mr. Matty, Aunt Batty, Patty and Natty, Mr. Hanratty, Fatty Cat, seventeen cans of paint, the stamps, the TV, the spaghetti, the bed, and all.

Maestro Ferlingatti and his string quartet were astonished by the colorful crowd that fell from the ceiling.

The Maestro loved an audience, even if they dropped in unannounced. But when Walter's bed smashed through the floor and paint splattered everywhere, the Maestro wished his audience would leave. And so they did, along with his string quartet.

Maestro Ferlingatti's practice room floor was also the basement ceiling. It was dark and quiet as midnight down there. Walter squeezed his eyes closed and tumbled through the darkness until he landed on something soft. . . .

He opened his eyes. Everything was in its place. His bedroom lights were out. The door was almost closed and through it Walter could hear his mother and father talking quietly.

"No more jumping on the bed for me," mumbled Walter as he lay back down to sleep.

Suddenly he heard a creak, the ceiling cracked, and down
came Delbert, bed and all. Down and down fell Delbert. . . .

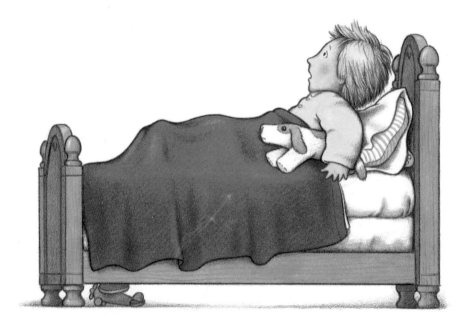